OASIS

Musings in Solitude

Alice Jomy

First Published in December 25 2023

Published by

KP INTERNATIONAL PUBLICATION

Published in London

113 Oakfield Road

London E61 LN

England.

Mob-0044 7940570677,

+91 9995153455

Foreword

Alice Jomy is now making a debut as a poet by publishing OASIS, a collection of her poems. Alice says that as an ordinary homemaker,she didn't have anything significant in her life to become a creative writer.

Born in 1952 in Kottayam ,married in 1974 flying to Ethiopia to join her husband Jomy Kuriakose in 1975 , blessed with three children and a brief career as a teacher in Nigeria , Alice couldn't dream of giving wings to her thoughts and ideas.....

Back home to Kerala, again she shut out her great passion for English and literature.

Misfortunes come and go, but life also holds surprises under its fold. A brief notification in the news paper announcing a meeting of 'Aksharasthree,The Literary Woman' in the year 2016 was indeed a breakthrough.

Thanks to all those who are taking steps to publish the book 'Oasis' . This will make her cherished dream come true, her silent wish to be an author ever since she has joined 'Aksharasthree'.

Alice as a writer is able to look into what is within herself, look back at the filaments of life , deal with love, loss, lamentations of the soul and find solace by rising on the wings of fancy. She finds peace and cheer in the oasis it offers.

May the verses penned by Alice Jomy provide every reader a poetic delight.

Prof.Leela Mary Koshy

Acknowledgements

This book of poems ' OASIS ' is my long cherished dream come true. On this memorable occasion, it is my privilege to express my love and gratitude to all those who made it possible for me.

As a God fearing person, I praise God for letting me hold this book as His precious gift to me. It has come as a balm.

My deep appreciation goes to Dr. Anniamma Joseph, the Founder President of 'Aksharasthree: The Literary Woman' . She has brought together women interested in creative writing, giving them a platform to express their talents.

I am also indebted to Prof.Lathaprem Sakhya, Dr.Daisy Jose and Prof.Prasanna Kumari ('Neelanilav') for their unstinted encouragement. My heart goes out to Prof.Leela Mary Koshy, who repeatedly advised me to publish a collection of my poems.

I am deeply indebted to Prof. Leela Mary Koshy for her timely editorial suggestions and also for her help with her superb literary skills.

There are many others who contributed to make 'OASIS ' a reality; with due respect for their wish to remain anonymous, let me mark this occasion with my informal 'Thank you' to all who helped in their own big and small ways.

Alice Jomy

Contents

OASIS

Walking through the barren desert,

feet swollen with hurting burns,

I looked up into the cloudy sky,like Hagar...

Darker than the sky was the

darkness within.....

Tears rolling down the cheeks,I gazed vacantly..

And then heard a voice so sweet from within;

The Voice whispered :

" Turn to the Most High! "

The sudden flash removed the darkness

within..

It showed an oasis in the forlorn desert !

Sweet smelling springs flowed,quenching my thirst !

Divine warmth enveloped me;

The frozen gloom within melted away !

There stood I drenched by the Living Spring !

My Inspirer

Noble she looks with her bobbed white hair

not so tall, not so short

Her   fragile figure spreading positive vibes all around..

Bold and self willed, bubbling with energy

Kind and sympathetic but stern and strict when needed…

Man or women sure to fall for her magical smile

Revealing her inner beauty,brilliance and caliber

Long to have her as my friend,philosopher and

guide for ever and ever

NAY, NOT I, BUT THEE, THE INFINITE

When the maddening crowd turns me crazy

When the weather is turbulent and the flight is about to crash

When the alarm ringtones of this mechanical mess frightens me...

I seek solace in the soothing hugs of

solitude

To have a glimpse of the mountain peak..

So remote , distant and out of reach

And coverd with glazing slippery snow..

To taste the mystical moments of celestial bliss..

Shutting the doors of senses and opening up the inner eye

At least for a tiny fraction of a moment..

Forgetting the embroidered costume worn,. with egoistic desires,

Presumed mistakenly as "I" ,

To be attuned to the boundless, limitless miraculous cosmic energy.

Our cosy space

Let us be crazy and elope

To an enchanted island

And find a cosy space in a haunted castle

Hidden amongst thick jungle

And there I will give you my virgin love

As pure as budding Jasmines

When fragrant breeze hugs us

Whispering the secrets of wild blossoms

And we will dance to the tune of your rythmic breathing

When lightning from your lustful eyes

Illuminates the dance floor

And the intoxicating odour of your sweat

Turns me into a bewitching nymph.

The Secret Cave

A space so holy deep within

To hide from the chasing,

Maddening crowd!

Chanting sacred Mantras

Unknown to the whole world

And be with you my love.

Enveloped in the soothing rays

Of your mesmerizing eyes

When the fragrance of your

Sweet smelling sweat

Turns my soma sense and

Soul into total bliss .

Home

Home was once an enchanted island

with a thousand blazing suns

and eternal spring with fragrance divine

The God I adorned in the sacred shrine

blessed me with wings to fly in a crazy sky...

but on a cloudy dark night

the Deity vanished into the thin air

leaving a vacuum which can never never be filled...

the encircling darkness scares me

in this forlorn desert

where I move like a zombie

with unstable steps

to some dubious mirage..

The cosmic dance

Millions and millions of galaxies

dancing to the rhythm of a mysterious tune

the choreography beyond our comprehension

perfect and precise to the minutest details

loyal and unfailing attraction

the theme of the music...

We the humans the inhabitants of this tiny blue dot

have a short stay here

to be joyful or miserable

and we make love and make our petty quarrels

unaware of this great cosmic dance of love!!!

Reflection

It was enchanting to see my reflection in his inviting eyes.

Those memories still turn the pitch black midnights into mesmerising moonlit euphoria..,

but... the luminous lunar delight disappears when the dazzling dawn arrives..

Now I seek my reflection in the tranquil pool deep within

and find solace in reflective contemplation.

Is it not idiotic to look into a mirror to see my reflection..?

It deceives with the perishable accessories of life.

It is better to reflect on the perpetual percevier deep within ..,

to be illuminated with the ultimate truth, The Eternal Bliss, 'Ananda'.

Deja vu

He stood tall and dark with a short beard

not so handsome like romantic heroes

but stout and erect like an African king..

wonder struck by the sudden intimacy with a total stranger

lost the well kept sense and sensibiliy,

reliving the past..

sweet kisses , warm hugs,

the intoxicating odour of his sweat

and the lust filled taste of his saliva in my mouth

so familiar..so mesmerising...

triggering a tremor, the magical feeling of dejavu vu

shifted us to an enchanted island

where law of love prevailed.

Jamais vu

The far away look in your eyes

caused a shudder in me...

Was it not yesterday that

we held hands and watched

the flame red sun drowning in the ocean..

Yet you sat there like a statue

with a blank stare..

Was it just an unforseen moment of jamais vu...?

Or a painful dismisal from your life...?

The New Found Love

We met too late my darling

The intoxicating fragrance of jasmines

Rekindles an ancient fire long lost

The sweetest encounter shifted me

To an enchanted planet

Where I met fairies with golden wings

Dancing above the ground.

Let me plant all the precious seeds

I have gathered so far.

Hoping the weather conducive for healthy growth.

And water them with my frozen tears

Yes, the warmth of my new found love

Sure to melt the passions frozen deep within.

Once upon a time...

Once upon a time, she too had a dream

A dream of bronze, painted with platinum and gold

Decorated with diamonds and sapphires..

The not so silly girl played with her dreams, to fly like a kite.

But the kite got stuck on the branches of an ancient tree

Never to be seen again.

Once upon a time,she too had a castle in a virgin jungle

Made of fragrant flowers so rare

The fire that swallowed the fauna and flora

Didn't spare her castle too.

But the multicolored rainbow up there in the sky

Winked at her, blessing her with wings to fly

To the wonderland of perpetual ease

And from there she got the grace to translate

Vacant gazes into captivating smiles

Furnaces into icy pools and agonies into ecstasies.

Memories

Sweet or bitter, memories are treasures

Carefully kept in a castle deep within

.Is it not a pilgrimage for the solitary soul

In a melacholic mood

To be in the treasure house

And cuddle the antique curios

Collected during the journey called life ?

Caressing the fondly cherished Gems

And reliving the bygone days, is a secret ritual

Chanting sacred Mantras unknown to the whole world.

Feel so empty

Feel so empty like a beer can

Content leaked out unnoticed

And lost the intoxicating attraction

Feel so empty like a perfume bottle

Broken into pieces and the fragrance spread into

the air and wasted

Feel so empty like a vacant house

The inhabitants dead and

gone

Feel so empty like a woman's womb

The budding life terminated

For fear of blaming eyes

Feel so empty like a Mama bird

Nest and eggs fell apart when the tree was cut

Feel so empty in and out

And all over for moments few or for ever..?

Soul sisters

We met as budding blossoms in our teens

When.dews on roses smiled and sparkled,winking at us

And romance and Romeos

Seemed like riddles to solve.

Her mischievous smile and dreamy eyes

Filled a vacant space in me.

Wondering at the kindred spirit seldom seen ..

Books and chess acted as glues.

Trekking through the virgin jungles

New found fançies felt so dear

But jealousy filled the blaming eyes

And put on the attire of advice in abundance

Turning us into rebellious teens.

Full blown blossoms plucked and packed

To be in strager's life to merge and melt.

.There we thrived and spread the fragrance

Tending our own gardens with love and zeal.

But still we feel like adolescent girls

When we meet and share our secrets.

The wrinkled skin and whitish hair

Did nothing to extinguish the fire within.

Weird Visions

An ancient castle, haunted and deserted

In a strange planet, unknown to the whole world!

There I sat on a half burned window

Brooding on the bygone days

Of family gatherings, feasting and rejoicing

On all a sudden ,the outside drama caught my eyes

Dipping me into a sadated daze

Strange creatures all around

Occult rituals done with haste

Reddish smoke of hellish smell

Zombies dance with lethargic sway

and around their opened grave

Vampires run with deadly speed

To quench their thirst for human blood

Galloping unicorns appear like lightning

Deadly Dinosaurs rule the land

Fighting with their might and main.

Scared and bewildered I sat like a rock

Knowing not what else to do!

A gentle touch and melodious voice

Brought me back to my senses sane

There you stood with a mesmerizing smile

Sparkling stars in your dreamy eyes

Sealing our love with a sensual kiss

Carried me back to our enchanted cave.

Hollow

How do we paint war; the deadly and tragic endeavour..?

With red , the colour of blood,

Or with black,the colour of mourners at the funeral...?

What is the sound of victory ?

The echoes of hellish lamentations...

Then why do we opt for the hollow victory

Believing in the hollow promises of some megalomaniacs..?

Better listen to the divine music

from the hollow flute..

To soothe the turbulent sea deep within..

And collect the pearls and leave the shells hollow,

To enrich and enlighten this voyage called life..

You too Brutus..

So hard to believe that you too can be a Brutus

So hard to digest the stones, I have swallowed..

Wandering though a forlorn desert

Weary and depressed, I was about to give up my search

And wither away like a leaf in winter.

Suddenly the music from a magical flute enchanted me

Shocked as it turned out to be a mirage

A thousand volcanoes erupted deep within

But life persists even after earthquakes and tsunamies

The vibrations bestowed upon me a refined consciousness

And the queen now is safe in the ivory tower.

Unbearable Parting

How can l part with you my darling

The separation unbearable

Like pricking thorns under my feet

And biting ants all over my body.

Haven't you learned that we are inseparable?

Then why are you in a coma

To be admitted far away.

Far away from me in a stranger's care?

Really scared how they would manipulate your

internal organs

Without damaging your friendly disposition..

Come back my beloved safe and sound in mind

and body

Oh, my beloved 'Samsung Galaxy J. 6+"

Ode to joy

Where do I meet Thee my love

In flavours of flesh or in my rosary beads ?

Didn't I search you in churches and temples…?

But you evaded me playing hide and seek

Climbing this slippery mountain called life

It dawned on me..

The choice is mine; to be joyful or miserable

And I prefer you my beloved…

The gloomy nights with thunder and lightning over..

Dawn arrives sprinkling sweet tears of happiness pure..

Blossoms spread colourful petals,

To give you a Red Carpet Welcome,

And the long cherished hugs shift us to a fascinating

fairy land.

The Garden of Love

If I knew your secret sleeping hut

I would come to you in this scary midnight

Spreading fragrance of my jasmine coloured virgin love

While clouds clash to illuminate

The darkest corners of my forlorn path.

If I had a mirror to see the depth of your heart

I could read your silence

Which burns me like a furnace.

Suppose I saw a barren desert there,

I would plant my dreams and water it with my tears,

To turn it into a mesmerising garden of love.

Solace

Scary storm and turbulent sea

Gigantic waves to swallow my tiny canoe

Come to me,my darling in your flying carpet

And take me to our magical cave

To find solace in each other's arms

Filling the air with fragrance of love

While the intoxicating odour of your warm sweat

Turns me into a bewitching nymph.

Painful Silence

Sitting alone,eyes half closed in a trance

Under a tamarind tree,

You looked like Budha

about to be enlightened.

But your silence,more eloquent than a soliloquy,

Expressing the turbulence deep within

Hurt me like a thousand thorns

As sharp as needles..

Rain

Blazing sun and burning mind

Heated furnace inside and outside

Sudden changes and shift in moods

As if nature too has bipolar disorder.

Clouded sky and scary thunder

The God of light disappears so fast

The waiting is over

And blessings showered as soothing raindrops

To cool the earth and calm the mind.

Wishful Thinking

Dreaming of a new world where the radience of love

melting away the frozen tears

of the voiceless masses..

and the fragrance of fraternity

wiping out the stinky disparities...

An uptopian dream I cherish always,

for this pale blue dot ,in the vast universe.

Moments of Ecstasy

As he carried her like a Barbie doll

to the flowery bed to shower

sweet sweet kisses on her starving lips

covering her with goosebumps

time hid behind the curtain, knowing not what else to do

and the envious moon peeped through the widow

with a reluctant smile,

when stars twinkled with delight

turning time and space irrelevent.

Whispering Streetlight

Illuminating even the darkest corners,not so forlorn

swallowing a thousand secrets unknown to the maddening masses

the yawning streetlight smiles mischievously in the morning

pondering on the strange whispers hidden in its belly..

The inviting smiles of the harlots and eunuch

waiting for their prey,

counting and calculating the monetary benefits,

and the thugs conspiring against their absent enemies,

the street dwellers competing for their little space

on the varandas of locked up shops...

and the bleeding two wheeler traveller

hit by flying vehicles of drunk drivers

pains its belly like undigested intakes.

A perplexing dilemma

All alone in this beautiful planet

strange creatures all around

searching in vain for my own species

the frustration hard to bear ..

like a thousand needles

pricking at once ,deep in the core...

masked faces all around

hard to identify friends and foe

no way to reject the coins so plenty

an impossible task to segragate genuine from fake..

better be a magnet of virtues

to attract only the genuine , valuable and precious.

The castaway

Gloomy midnight attired in pitch black burka

Mounting chaos all-around and deep within

Am I not a castaway in a barren desert island

Not even a twinkling firefly as a glimmer of hope

Still dare to fancy the arrival of the armoured prince riding on a unicorn

To illuminate my dreams with butter milk moons and twinkling stars

to carry me to an enchanted island

to be in eternal spring

Where fragrant roses dance to the rhythm of our jingling giggles,winking
mischievously

And the sky above celebrates our reunion witth fire works of thunder and
lightning.

Midnight dreams

When this marvellous blue marble is covered in black,

Like an alluring maiden attired in Burka,

When the owl calls for its mate with lustful fancies,

When everyone swings in the cradle of silence and slumber,

Meet me in my midnight dreams , my love,

And wipe away my burning tears of wounded memories,

Turning the pitch dark midnight into the splendor of a thousand blazing suns

Growing Older

Graying hair and growing hindsight

Sagging breasts and swollen knees

Aching back and diminishing eyesight

The costume gets spoiled bit by bit

The Precious Gem preserved without blemish

In the perishable shell, invisible and everlasting

A tiny spark from the' Most High'

Radiates the celestial glow without any flaw

Brightening awareness and insights while growing older

Lightening even the darkest moments of despair.

SEASONS

Seasons arrive in varied moods

smiling ,laughing, shouting, and crying

blessing the earth with fragrance and voluptuousness

gifting costumes of varied hues and textures

not always with multicolored floral designs of a bride,

a widow's plain white dress, sure to be worn with gloomy eyes..

seasons of life too celebrated

with cuisine of differing tastes,

sweet , bitter, hot and sour.

ROCKS

Be my rock , I pleaded with sobs

but you stood there like a rock

watching the sea breathing in anger

against the nude rocks without mosses

and she came and held your hands

whispering in you ears " Let's rock"

brooding over our relationship on rocks

I found solace in whiskey on rocks.

Dead Leaves

No way to cling to the bough

when the time is ripe,

a journey back to the mother earth,

from where everything sprouts and springs up...

Did fallen leaves too have

hidden secrets of shattered dreams,

rainbow colored dreams that had accidentally fallen apart..?

You

Haven't you heard the mesmerising music from my flute..?

Haven't you seen the blazing flame of my burning love...?

Haven't you sensed the fragrance of a thousand blooming roses...?

Then, why can't you ignore your oscillating emotions, And come down from your mountain peak,

To the alluring green meadows to be in bliss

In a secluded sweet smelling thatched hut...?

Reunion

She came to me limping

like a wounded deer

The salty flow from her vacant eyes

Burned her cheeks like a spring too hot

as she wiped it with a tiny hanky...

The swollen knees aching and reddish

Hurting her like her aching broken heart

The greying hair and sagging breasts

Seemed like the debris of an ancient beauty...

Bewilded I remained standstill for a while

The girl so cheerful like a succulent rose

Smiled at me in the threshold of my memory

The fragrance that she spread around

soothing balm to to many lonely souls

And her loving hugs were healing touch

For many a neglected and needy hearts

But wed lock turned as lock of jail

Extinguishing the fire in her

Like railway tracks they never met or merged

And lived as strangers till he left

I stood numb as if in a trance for a while
Till her embrace locked us together
And the heavens showered its blessings as icy drops
While God of light smiled at us mirthfully.

Healing The Universe

Break the cocoons

and flutter like butterflies

purify the rotten minds

with love and

compassion

let joy and hope prevail

over dismay

wipe out the conflicts

and heal the soul

rewrite the destiny

of the universe

for universe is

within us.

Hidden Treasures

Caressing my hidden treasures is a ritual
to sustain me in the jim jams of this journey called life...
a pocket full of posies to fight the foul odour
when rotten debris of memories
peep through window curtains....
a pocketful of buttermilk moon
to tranquilize me when I go crazy out of the blue..
a pocketful of rainbows to charm me,
when life seems colourless and boring
and a pocketful of sunlight
to lead me to my destination , when flying solo
through pitch black midnights of turbulant moments.

Greener Planet

Though,mere pop ups in this vast cosmos,

promted by our boosted ego and mounting arrogance,

the ecosystem is mishandled ,polluted

disturbed and destroyed ...

boomaraging continues as

the smoke filled air , acid rains,

triggering land slides and insane tsunamis ....

Let's pacify the revolting mother earth by going green, toiling for a greener planet.

Wild Fantasies

Gazing back

through the mirrors

of time ,

the wild fantacies

of bubbling

pre- teen days of yore;

a longing to sail

on the clouds and

be attired

with a piece of the rainbow

seems so magical

and alluring still.

Language

He stood transfixed gazing into my eyes

Like the statue of Eros breathing heavily with unruly passions..

I was spellbound...like a frozen thunder..

Do we need to embrace the linguistics

to perceive the language of

the ceseless ripples of reminiscences...?

Has anyone designed the aphabets for the language

of the whisperings of fragrant breeze

or for the blooming blossoms'

mesmerizing smiles..?

Arise

Arise, Oh lovely ladies

hold hands and stand together ;

break the thorny chains

and open the cages,

let's fly beyond the icy clutches

of jealousy and vainly boosted ego

and dream of a world of eternal spring..

though women are like rose petals,

soft and emotional

still hard and blazing like diamonds..

woman is a stunning mystery unsolved,

she absorbs all the shocks

but never breaks

and endures to win ,not to fall apart.

Touch

A soothing balm to the wounded heart

if perfumed with love and care,

a tranquilizer to sedate the depressed,

when lamenting in agony ,unbearable .

A healing touch radiates the divine glow,

a panacea for misery hidden deep within ,

and the sensul touch of a genuine lover

to unearth the feminine charm,

transports the innocent maiden,

to unknown domains of ecstasy .

My Rainbow

A soothing ark of a sparkling rainbow

sprang up on my inward sky

spontaneously turning into

a stunning semi- circular colour magic

wiping away the blues and glooms,

ferrying freshness and fragrance,

fashioning my inner world

with a colourful spring...

and the golden horizon I behold,

fascinates me beyond my wildest fantasy.

Nothing to hide

Your love is like a burning furnace

that purifies the ugly blemishes in me

your love is like the refreshing radiance of a thousand blazing suns

wiping away the encircling darkness

from my sorrowful solitary soul...

and I stand before you, stark naked

for I have nothing to hide from you my love.

Smiles

Smiles are like blooming flowers with varied hues

Spreading fragrance all around.

The celestial smiles of newborn babes

As pure as dews on green grass,

Wipe away the blemishes of adult minds.

Captivating smiles brimming with exuberance,

Mesmerising smiles perfumed with love,

Inviting smiles embroidered with burning desire,

Lazy smiles attired in rejection,

Weary smiles filled with sorrow,

And vacant smiles of shattered dreams,

Transport us into unknown terrains and unforseen moods.

EUPHORIA

It is euphoric to hide

in an enchanted cave,

a cosy space deep within,

to forget the jim- jams

of the maddening word,and be in bliss, with you my love,

when the lightning from your mesmerising eyes

wipes away the darkness

from my soul.

The Frozen Passoins

With his first sensual kiss

the posies of passions bloomed

and the lazy breeze

spread the fragrance with a mischievous wink...

feasting on the nectar the honey bees danced

celebrating the moments of love the blossoms and beetles forgot themselves in ectacy...

.All on a sudden the earth triggered..

everything cracked and broke into pieces...

hearing lost with the heavy thunder

sight lost with the unbearable flash of lightning...

The Diety diappeared

and passions froze like iceberg

under the vast blue ocean.

Myself

A tiny spark of the divine

blemished by carnal passions,

lost in hurricanes and sand dunes,

still, seeking for the celestial fragrance

and elegant splendor deep deep within ,

unique ultimate and unparalleled..

though paradoxically like a drop of water,in the vast blue ocean ,

when lightning of enlightening burns the duality into ashes..

Arrogance

How can you shout at me like a monster

With dreadful thunder from your mouth..?

How can you abuse me like an enemy

With sharp knife on your tongue..?

How can you stare at me like a criminal

With burning fire in your eyes...?

How can you disown me like a stranger

With cold frozen indifference..?

How can you change like a chameleon

With colours unimaginable all over..?

How can you drive like a lunatic..?

Yes, I know,it is only mounting rage

awful arrogance and nasty snobishness.

Society

A lady in white wearing a mask of georgeous smile

reddish lipstick glittering

with uptopian ideas of

freedom,fraternity and equality

but her under garments emitting ,

stinky odour of dirty cheating

and disparities in abundance

Words

A soothing balm to the burning mind

and a healing touch to the wounded soul

but a sharp tongue, like a heavy hammer

breaks the heart into pieces.

Sweet or bitter, words reveal the inner self..

so taming the tongue is a stepping stone

to explore and conquer

the gigantic mountain of peace and harmony.

Autum Leaf

Falling not with regrets

but leaving the stage

when the role is over

with a contented smile on the lips

waiting gracefully for the final call..

reminding us of the futility

of the fleeting pleasures

and the fulfiment of a fruitful life..

a feast for the eyes ,

with colours dazzling,

the autum leaves turn us spellbound

like the setting sun so spendid.

Vanquished hopes

A flight in the mid air,

visibility low and weather turbulant.. .

Is it not what we celebrate

as life in this tiny blue dot...?

a frightening reality making us insecure frequently..

but vanquished hopes rise again from the ashes like Phoenix

and lightning ,crashing the clouds of dreams,

brightens even the darkest moments,

making a safe landing

wrapping soma sense and soul

with goosebumps of gleeful grace.

Miracle

What is not a miracle on this planet ..?

the mesmerising grin of a lover

changing a naive girl into a passionate princess ..

the innocent smile of a newborn babe

turning a woman into an ever loving fearless mom..

and the naughty grandchild's tantrums

viewed as the most enjoyable entertainment

by the weak and bored grand parents..

yes ,whatever happens through out this short stay here,is a miracle

if we have curious eyes and amused gaze.

A woman fearless

A budding life in the womb

surely a miraculous previlage

to dance to the tune of the creator

a naive girl uplifted to a woman fearless

to protect , stand with and fight

for her sweet little one ever after

the envious master enslaves her

to boost his tarnished ego.

Yardsticks of folly

A wonderful journey from womb to tomb

baggages of blessings and burdens plenty to carry

better be a witness till the curtain falls

when turbulent weather and raging storms

gift us with a scary voyage..

and blaming eyes measure us with their own Yardsticks

yardstics of folly with utterly foolish measurement.

My reflection

Do I need a mirror to see my reflection?

It deceives with the perishable accessories of life

better reflect on the perpetual percevier deep within

to be illuminated with the ultimate truth, The Eternal Ananda.

Dreaming in loneliness

A castaway lost in a desert island

mounting chaos deep within

gloomy midnight attired in pitch black burka

not even a firefly to light up the night

still fancy buttermilk moons and glimmering stars to illuminate my dreams

when the twinkle of a cherished memory radiates waves of joy deep within,

turning the barren desert into a mesmerising garden in spring.

Confused and crazy

Can't process this volcanic eruption deep within...

and solve the perplexing puzzle creditably..

a thousand solutions fluttering like butterflies..

turning me confused and crazy...

how can I recapture my serenity..

to perceive the scenario with clarity..?

Counting

No point in counting the wounds and scars,

Do spiders count the failed jumps while making spider webs ?

Celebrate life without any care,

like fluttering butterflies enjoing the short span,

for each day break is span new.

The now and here

Kiss me now and here, my darling

to savour the sweetness for ever..

delete the memories of the roaring seas of yesterdays

and survive the upcoming tempests of tomorrows..

for now and now only beget the fragrance sure and certain.

New Beginnings

Each Dawn arrives like a newly wed bride

spreding love and light, bestowing an enchanting mood,

to have fresh beginnings with brand new dreams like scarlet red roses...

the blooming blossoms are mesmerising

with dews

but, the same old roots sustain the survival.

Spring

When pushed into life's barren deserts , as fait accompli,

what else to do but to fancy the fragrance of spring all around

with the soothing presence

and healing touch of the Almighty

and look squarely at the pitch black midnight

awaiting the mesmerizing dawn in spring as my raison d' etre.

Thoughts

Burning thoughts burst

and erupt like volcanoes

causing havoc dreadful and unbounded.

Pacifying the thundering mind

to be silent and still to taste the thoughtless void,

opens up new dimensions

of previously alien realms:

a mountain peak covered with slippery snow

so remote and distant reserved only for mystics.

Looking back

Was it not yesterday that I floated with clouds

My attire embellished with stars

And rode on unicorn to find treasures hidden in the horizon..?

When did I fall to this rotten debris of shattered dreams..?

Or, is it a dream within a dream..?

Or an untrodden snowy path to my own Shangri LA...?

Solo traveller

Is it not euphoric to meet the inner eagle deep within and soar,

to savour the ecstasy of flying solo..?

why not enjoy voyage en solitaire

for planets too are solo travellers...

My space

Do I have a spce of my own in this privilaged existence

when I am conscious of the   vanishing duality...?

Are we not just pop ups in this vast cosmos...

unaware of the truth that time and space are persistent illusions..?

Do I need to be enlightened to perceive the ultimate truth..

" the universe is within me "...?

New year

New year arrives like a serpentine beauty,

winking mischievously

with an intriguing smile on her rainbow coloured face

Her hugs and kisses only will decode

the mysteries hidden in her winking eyes and mysterious gaze..

May her fresh fragrance be the same

through out the year and ever and ever...

Love

Love..genuine love ,the spice of life

panacea for the painful disharmony with cosmic rhythm..

Is it not the scuba when diving deep down

the ocean of birth and rebirth..

to fetch the treasures so precious and rare

and taste the sweetness of honey like undercurrents of hidden passions.

Please

Like the smile on our lips when we meet

like the warmth in our hearts when we greet

like the diamonds that glitter on the bracelet

like the music that is heard from the anklets

the constellation of six letters called PLEASE

has an aura that can't be rejected

when making an appeal

melting even the hardest rock of a heart.

Sleepwalk

When the facinating blue dot

is attired in pitch black burka

I find my keys hidden delibrately

to open the secret doorways

to my own Shangri-La

to sleepwalk with Apsaras and Gandharvas

and recapture the serenity lost

in the hurly burly of life.

Chains

Hard to break the enslaving chains

chains of the society and of the clergy

chains decorated with sharpened nails

Wounding the very core,

causing bleeding unstoppable ..

and the fragrant chains of love

with a golden tint ,adorned with diamonds

turns us crazy,witless

and at times soulless zombies.

Unspoken Words

Still remember

the unspoken words

of blazing suns in your

adolescent eyes

but you failed to read

the pregnant silence

in a budding flower...

drifted apart as

far away planets

in the vast galaxies

without a big bang...

sometimes

a momentary rainbow

flashes in the crazy sky

as reinitiation of

teenage memories.

Covid 19: Lock down

Lip lock kisses suspended

spiritual centers closed

entertainments curtailed

streets and shops empty

cutthroat competion diappeared

the whole world at a standstill

as in Sleeping Beauty's fairy tale

the princess will be kissed

and everything will restart

all on a sudden.

Life's little surprises

The moon walking with a naughty boy pestering his mom

the firefly twinkling in the new moon night,feasting his eyes

the dews dancing on the morning grass like dazzling diamonds

the beauty of the fluttering butterflies and swaying peacocks

the amazing glimmer in the eyes of an adolescent lover

celebrating the opening ceremony of sensual pleasures...

without these little surprises

wouldn't life be a barren desert

lacking the charms and hues of an enchanting spring..?

Day dreams

A mysterious fairy land of eternal spring

where time and space have no relevence

free from the cluches of clergy's strange dicta

and stragling laws of corrupt authorities

away from moral policing and prying eyes

a paradise in the midst of turbulant war zone called life

crossroads

Hold my hand and lead me

my unfailing love and light

to celebrate the freedom

of the reborn

when staying rooted,

confused and jaded

on the Crossroads of life

for Thy Will is my wish and

Thy decision,my destination.

Another step on my ladder

When seized by dizzy spells while climbing the ladder to reach the summit ,

if next step looks like an impossible task,

and quitting seems the only choice,

hold His hands surrendering to His will

and leap to the apex fearlessly,

to own the treasures awaiting in plenty.

Thunder

The sky above gazing down

with glaring eyes

muttering clouds turn crazy,

slamming into one another-

enemies when temper lost,

thundering war cries fill the air,

as fireballs signal the start..

The terrified earth shudders !

knowing not what else to do,

accepting the soothing shower

as tears of regret,

to be in love once again,

when sanity is regained..

I love

When the darkening sky

scares me with fire crackers

when the mischievous clouds,

attired in varied hues

chase one another in playful moods

I love feasting my eyes

with the beauty of the celestial celebration,

listening to your rhythmic breathing,

entrapped in your warm embrace.

Open the door

Waiting for you my darling,

waiting and waiting for the syphonic sound of your horse hoof..

come , and open the closed doors

of my inner castle deep within..

with your secret key of crazy passion

steal a glance at the rooms of spectacular opulance

Oh my love ! my everlasting love,

cross the threshold and

claim the treasures untouched

and let's dance to the tune of the tempests in our hearts..

Bliss

When perception blossoms with divine fragrance,

decoding the mysteries of existence ,

wiping away the blemished illusion of duality,

Unearthing the mystic hidden under the selfish self,

When the mirrors of time and space are broken,

When one turns orgasmic without the need of enslaving pleasures

The liberating peak of cosmic consciousness is attained ,

to be in perpetual bliss...the eternal Ananda..

The expressive eyes

Yesterday I looked into your expressive eyes

to dig out a flash of secret desire

but there I could read only indifference

or was it hidden annoyance...?

And deep deep inside it hurt so bad..

bleeding still with unusual pain...

The sleepless night was quite an age

drowning in an empty sea..

my hurting heart still did hope

it hoped yearned,pined

for a change of mood in your expressive eyes.

The changing moods in your expressive eyes

like changing colours of a midsummer sky

sometimes bright sometimes dim

and sometimes dark as cloudy night...

Not as pools but like unpredictable sea

roaring and stormy yet can be silent and still...

I love watching those tides when we talk

but I love more to melt in you

when creamy foams glitter with sensual love.

An act of childhood

Memories of childhood seems like magnificent rainbows of yore..

still, measles smallpox and whoopingcough escaped

when Pandora's box was slightly opened..

and paradise lost, when frowning pediatricians opted for injections

but paradise regained when smiling homoeopaths

gave sweet sweet tiny white dainties

wiping away the fear so consuming..

The Golden Peak

The golden peak of perpectual bliss

an enticing dream of every seeker..

the narrow path and constant storm clouds

scare the reluctant and lazy seekers

but the alluring aroma encircling the dream spot,

inviting ,enchanting,everlasting

and hard to ignore ...

Turning inward to seek and find the treasures

is indeed a solo flight facinating,

thrilling and invigorating.

The untrodden path

Is it not thrilling to take

the untrodden path

covered with slippery snow

for it leads to the wild

exuberance of existence...?

unveil the unknown

to have a glimpse of the mysteries

of this journey called life

in this facinating pale blue dot.

Dreams

A ray of hope for the melecholic

a thousand blazing suns for the reformer

a mesmerizing island for lovers

and a vacant spce for the lazy.

Building bonds

Do we need to build bonds ...?

bondings evolve sponaniosly like blooming blossoms...

enjoy watering the seedling with affection and trust

and celebrate the intimacy as the finest fortune.

When ink fights

Neither blak nor blue

not even green

when ink fights, it is red

the colour of blood

which sustains life..

sharper than sword ,

the revolting pen

conquering the conscience,

awekening the dormant minds.

My Teacher

The silver moon shows the lonely traveller his way;

The blazing sun blesses

the wicked and virtuous alike;

The cool,cool torrents quench the thirst of this lovely blue dot.

It's a feast to the flora and fauna and the arrogant humans as well!

Ahwa! Teach me to be humble, humane and full of compassion;

Remind me always that we're mere pop ups in this universe.

I bow before thee, Nature, my Great Teacher!

Thou art mysterious, unpredictable and fraught with riddles in thy very essence!

Yet I bow to thee, Oh, Nature!

Silence

Read my silence if you can

Pregnant silence with burning desire

Frozen emotions sweeter than ice cream ...

Melt it with warm warm kisses

Haven't you seen the spark in my eyes..?

And the blossoming roses on my starving lips 💋 ...?

Inner Child

Children we are still , deep deep within

longing to be petted patted pampered

kissed and hugged...

to be once again, the ever adored princess of

"Daddy The Great"

recapturing the sweet moments in fantasy to enjoy,

sheer euphoric shower in a secret paradise .

A change in the air

Yes, no way to row forward..

my little canoe about to break..

everything falling apart all on a sudden..

come to me , my darling in your flying carpet

take me to your enchanted island

where nightingales sing to welcome us

and wild jasmine and roses smile at us

telling the tale of a new order

filling the air with love and care

blazing with positive vibes.

Love in isolation

The evening breeze whispers to me

about your love laden heart

the sudden shower wets me

with your tears of separation ..

the same moonlit night intoxicates us,

although we are far away..

to ward off bitterness

caused by unfulfilled desires,

I find solace in colourful imagination...

and the magic of fantasy

overwhelms me

in these gloomy days of isolation

Intuition

Like lightning it dawn on the mind's eye

Logic withdraws with a sigh

Reasoning sabotaged mysteriosly

The magical rhythm of cosmic music

Tunes up the whispering of the soul.

Wisdom capable of overpowering intelligence

Furnished data and details flutter like butterflies

And then stay still

Opening up an intruiging dimension beyond...

Like a canine's knowledge about Tsunamies beforehand,

Like the unstoppable barking

Forseeing the upcoming dangers..

A disturbence within without reason

A decision taken without cosent

A higher sense beyond our comprehension

Directing us at a time of overwhelming uncertainity.

Colourful pieces of memory

Holding the hands of my bestie

running to a forlorn corner of the playground

to share our innermost secrets of adolescence,

the musical giggles of our colourful glass bangles

and the rainbows in her innocent eyes

and the blooming blossoms on her not so red lips..

a colourful piece of memory;

which transports me to a planet with eternal spring..

My ancestral home

Lingering memories of a bygone era

still sweet and fresh like

the breeze from the paddy fields...

women transplanting paddy, with only wrappers to cover their nakedness...

and men breathing heavily beside their women...

the intoxicating musky smell of their sweat....

celebrations of harvest festivals, the sound of the machetes..

their jovial songs with peculiar rhythms..

the odour of the cow dung from the cattle shed

crowing roosters and cooing pegions..

and my gradmother with her Rosary and " The Imitation of Christ"

the warmth of her loving kisses still fresh on my cheeks..

the ancient black and white nostalgic film continues...

Still I rise

Like the dormant embers

covered with ashes

ignite and turn into an inferno,

I too rise,

though shattering blows may

blow out the flame for a while..

Though crushed like sugercane

in this journey called life

I rise

burning the bagasses of weaknesses

and extracting the essense

with sugary flavour

to add to the sweet harmonious rhythm

of the innermost core of life.

If I were young again

If I were young again

I would burn my vanity

into ashes

To unveil the longings

unfulfilled..

Would sip from the vast

ocean of love

Swim naked like a

jovial mermaid

Without any care

And dive deep into the

depth of the ocean

To fetch my own treasures

left untouched.

Pickle and Wine

Sweet or bitter memories are treasures

sugary moments can be stored

like wine ,colourful and bubbling..

enjoy the delight ,sip by sip..

pickle the bitter events in a porcelain jar,

made of forgiveness unconditional ,

add salt and chillies of tolerance and care

pour the vinegar of ever flowing love

put some cumin seeds of humility..

keep in store till mellowed ..

ripples of reminiscences beget   solace in solitude.

Fragments of memory

Are we not kintsugi artists

joining the fragments of memories

with golden glue

transforming even the ugliest cuts and wounds

into fascinating recollections...?

accepting the cracks with grace

and forgiving onself

lift up the ripples of reminiscences

to enchanting and mystical orbits..